NOT SIT DOWN

by
Mara Rockliff

illustrated by
Ann Tanksley

Alfred A. Knopf ✦ New York

THIS IS A BORZOI BOOK PUBLISHED BY ALFRED A. KNOPF

Text copyright © 2012 by Mara Rockliff
Jacket art and interior illustrations copyright © 2012 by Ann Tanksley

All rights reserved. Published in the United States by Alfred A. Knopf, an imprint
of Random House Children's Books, a division of Random House, Inc., New York.

Knopf, Borzoi Books, and the colophon are registered trademarks
of Random House, Inc.

Visit us on the Web! www.randomhouse.com/kids

Educators and librarians, for a variety of teaching tools,
visit us at www.randomhouse.com/teachers

Library of Congress Cataloging-in-Publication Data
Rockliff, Mara.
My heart will not sit down / by Mara Rockliff ; illustrations by Ann Tanksley. — 1st ed.
p.   cm.
Summary: In 1931 Cameroon, young Kedi is upset to learn that children in her
American teacher's village of New York are going hungry because of the Great
Depression, and she asks her mother, neighbors, and even the headman for money to
help. Includes historical notes.
ISBN 978-0-375-84569-7 (trade) — ISBN 978-0-375-94569-4 (lib. bdg.) —
ISBN 978-0-375-98728-1 (ebook)
[1. Charity—Fiction. 2. Schools—Fiction. 3. Depressions—1929—New York (State)—
Fiction. 4. Cameroon—History—20th century—Fiction. 5. New York (N.Y.)—
History—1898–1951—Fiction.]
I. Tanksley, Ann, ill. II. Title.
PZ7.R5887My 2012
[E]—dc22
2011001117

The illustrations in this book were created using watercolor, pen and ink, and oils.

MANUFACTURED IN MALAYSIA
January 2012
10 9 8 7 6 5 4 3 2 1
First Edition

Random House Children's Books supports
the First Amendment and celebrates
the right to read.

To Lisa, who loves Africa
—M.R.

To John, Jane, Gail,
Donnie, Jillian, and Don
—A.T.

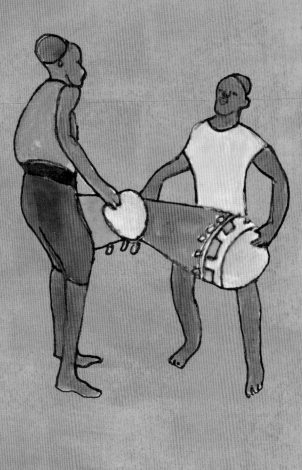

School day! School day!
Children, come—come—come!

Kedi hurried down the dusty path, her bare feet
moving to the call drum's quick, sharp beat. She did
not want to be late to school. She wanted to get a
good seat, close to Teacher. All the children liked to
sit near Teacher, so they could look at his strange black
shoes and watch the way his yellow mustache turned
up when he smiled.

But Teacher was not smiling today. He sat on a log, holding a paper, looking sad.

"Bad news from America," he said. "The Depression is getting worse."

America was his home, far away across the great salt river. Teacher told the children the Depression was a time of trouble for America. Like the sun scorching the earth in the season of burning feet, the Depression made everything good dry up and disappear. Men and women had no work to do. Children went hungry. In New York, he said, people were starving because they did not have money to buy food.

"Is that your village?" Kedi asked. "New York?"

Teacher smiled. "I suppose you could call it a village—
a very, very big village, with people from around the world."

All day, Kedi thought about the hungry children in New York, America, and her heart stood up for them in sympathy.

Kedi knew how it felt to be hungry. Many days, she had wished for a bit of meat when there was none. Many nights, she had emptied her bowl without filling her belly. Imagine how it would be to have no food at all!

"Why the sad face, little one?" said Mama as they worked together in the garden, harvesting peanuts and yams.

"Teacher said the people in his village have nothing to eat."

"Let them come to us," said Mama. "We will share."

"But they live very far away, across the great salt river. They cannot all come." Then Kedi had a new thought. "Teacher said they needed money to buy food. Could we give him money to send home?"

"Money!" said Mama. "We do not have enough coins to pay the head tax, even. How can we send money to people whose faces we have never seen?"

THE GREAT SALT RIVER

Kedi knew Mama was right. Still, her heart
would not sit down. *Someone in the village must
have money,* she thought. *I will go and ask.*
    Kedi asked the uncle squatting on the ground,
weaving a basket out of bush-rope vine.

She asked the sweeping mother with the baby
on her back and the grandmother with strong arms
pounding cassava.

She asked the laughing girls who carried pots
of river water balanced on their heads.

She asked the old men gathered under the thatched roof of the palaver house, playing their game of stones.

Finally, bowing her head and speaking softly into her cupped hands, she even asked the headman of the village.

Everywhere the answer was the same. Nobody had money to send far across the great salt river to America.

At home, Kedi helped stir the soup for supper.
She breathed in the spicy smell and sighed, thinking
of the children who could not look forward to a bowl
of soup with fou-fou and a bit of meat and greens.

When night came, she lay on the bamboo bed
between her brothers and sisters, but she could
not find sleep.

Sitting in the doorway, Kedi gazed into the
sky. Did the same bright stars, like twinkling
eyes, look down on hungry children
in New York, America?

In the morning, Kedi heard the distant beat of the drum calling *Come—come—come*. She started to run down the path to school.

Then Mama called her back. "Little one," she said,
"give this to Teacher, for the people in his village.
Tax time is not here yet. We will find a way."

Kedi stared down at the single small coin in her
palm. She knew Mama had no more to give. But
would it be enough?

"Thank you," she whispered, and turned away.
On the way to school, Kedi could not stop
peeking in her fist. Each time, the money
looked smaller, and her steps grew
slower.

Lessons had already begun. Kedi sat down in the back, far away from Teacher. She knew she should give him Mama's money right away, so it did not get lost. But she could not make herself speak.

Finally, she raised her hand. "Teacher, are there many children in New York?"

"Why, yes," he said, looking surprised.
"As many children as we have in our village?"
Teacher laughed. "Oh, many more," he said.
"In New York, the people crowd each other like
the tall grass in the field."
So many! Kedi felt her eyes fill up with tears.
How could she offer him her small, small money?

Then she heard the noise, *thump thump, thump thump,*
like the beat of a drum—the sound of many footsteps.

First the headman came.

Next came the men from the palaver house, and
after them, the uncle with his basket and the other men
and boys.

Then came all the women: grandmothers, young mothers with their babies, laughing girls.

Last of all came Mama.

"We have heard about the hunger in our teacher's village," said the headman. "Our hearts would not sit down until we helped."

One by one, the people went up with their
money, till it poured from Teacher's open hands.
Kedi's small, bright coin glittered among the rest.

"Well, little one," Mama said. "Now will your heart sit down in peace?"

Kedi thought about the children far across the great salt river in New York, America.

"Yes, Mama," she said. "Yes!"

AUTHOR'S NOTE

My Heart Will Not Sit Down was inspired by a true event. In 1931, the city of New York received a gift of $3.77 to feed the hungry. It came from the African country of Cameroon.

Many people in New York really were hungry at that time. The stock market had crashed in 1929, sending the nation into a depression. Factories closed by the thousands. Banks failed, wiping out people's life savings. Businessmen who lost their jobs ended up selling apples on a street corner for five cents apiece. Families that couldn't pay the rent were thrown out of their homes, and "breadlines" for soup kitchens stretched for blocks. Beggars everywhere asked, "Brother, can you spare a dime?"

Even at Depression prices, $3.77 wouldn't have gone very far in New York City. For the villagers in Cameroon who sent it, though, the money would have been a fortune. In fact, money played a very small role in their lives. Women grew food for their families (mainly corn, peanuts, yams, cassava root, and greens) in gardens beyond the villages. Men planted cacao trees, fished, and hunted in the jungle for anything they could spear, from wild pig to snake. They built their houses out of mud, and thatched the roofs with palm fronds. If they earned a little money, they spent it on basic items such as salt and metal tools, or payment of the "head tax" levied by British and French colonial authorities.

America was going through hard times, but life in Cameroon was always hard. Village girls like Kedi had no bicycles or toys. Instead, they spent their time working in the garden, hauling water, caring for younger brothers and sisters, and helping cook the family's one meal of the day over an open fire. Growing enough food to stay alive was a constant struggle, yet people shared with anyone in need. Even a stranger from far away was sure to be offered a meal and a bed. After all, as the villagers said, "You may meet him again, and in his own place."

How did people living without telephones or radios, so far from the United States, ever learn about the Great Depression and the suffering in New York City? Most likely, the news came from a teacher at one of the rural schools run by American missionaries. Because these schools were commonest in the south of Cameroon, the story is set there, among a southern ethnic group known as the Bulu.* In the story, the villagers use several Bulu expressions, including "the great salt river" (the Atlantic Ocean), "the season of burning feet," and, of course, "my heart stands up and it will not sit down." The Bulu are just one of Cameroon's hundreds of ethnic groups, each with its own language and customs. However, their way of life is typical of many rural villages in Cameroon and other parts of Africa during the time when this story takes place.

As for Kedi's belief that no one should ever go hungry, that belongs to the world.

It belongs to the children of a little town in Guatemala called Santo Domingo. Like Kedi, they came from poor families and they didn't always have enough to eat. But when they heard about hungry children in the African country of Malawi, they wanted to help. They

* The name Kedi is not Bulu, but Bafia. Kedi (pronounced *KAY-dee*) is the African name of Doris Anderson Reeves, who generously shared with me her experiences growing up in Cameroon at the time of this story.

went to the town soccer field after games and picked up aluminum cans people had left behind—900 cans in all. Then they sold the cans for $16, which they sent to feed the children in Malawi.

It belongs to the Papua New Guinea islanders who shared the greens from their gardens with American Peace Corps volunteers. Showing their hosts a photograph of New York City skyscrapers, the Americans mentioned the problem of homelessness. The islanders looked at the photo and clicked their tongues in astonishment—not at the height of the buildings, but at the idea of people living on the streets, begging for food. "We will write to your leaders," they said, "and tell them we will give these people land so they can grow food to eat."

It also belongs to all the soup kitchens, food banks, and other organizations that feed hungry people, and to the groups that work to solve the root causes of hunger.

It belongs to everyone whose heart will not sit down.